SPIRITUALS

MARK BOZZUTI-JONES

Augsburg Fortress
PUBLISHERS

SPIRITUALS

MARK BOZZUTI-JONES

Editors:
Jeffrey S. Nelson,
Elizabeth Drotning
Cover design:
Marti Naughton

Scripture quotations are from New Revised Standard Version Bible, copyright © 1989 Division of Christian Education of the National Council of the Churches of Christ in the United States of America. Used by permission.

Copyright © 2002
Augsburg Fortress
All rights reserved.
May not be reproduced.
ISBN 0-8066-4471-0
Manufactured in U.S.A.

05 04 03 02   1 2 3 4

Introduction 3

Were You There 7

Swing Low, Sweet Chariot 15

This Little Light of Mine 23

Let Us Break Bread Together 31

I Want Jesus to Walk With Me 39

Resources 47

Introduction

Welcome to Sing the Faith!

Welcome to *Spirituals,* one of six volumes in the Sing the Faith Bible study series. You are embarking on a biblical exploration of grace through the poetry, music, and history of five of the most beloved hymns of the Christian tradition.

Hymns are the faith people sing. The lyrics are owned by the people as the fabric of their theology. Many hymns have been in the memories of churchgoers for years. The melodies and texts of hymns are often retained after most other memory has faded. This series will allow participants to connect these well-loved hymns to biblical texts.

Pastors and worship leaders spend a significant amount of time searching for hymns related to the Sunday readings, the theme, and the mood of each service. Indexes are available to assist planners in coordinating biblical texts and songs. The Sing the Faith series brings this information and its powerful faith formation capability to you.

Each session focuses on one hymn. Participants will reflect on their personal history with the hymn, explore biblical connections in the texts, learn the history and legends associated with the hymn, and consider how the message of the hymn applies to their daily journey of faith.

Preparing your study

The Sing the Faith series, designed for small-group Bible study, encourages interaction among participants to help them grow and enrich their journeys of faith. Alternate groupings, with minor modifications, would be possible. Individuals might use this resource for personal study or partner with another individual to study and correspond by phone or e-mail.

The thematically connected hymns in each volume can be studied at any time and in any church season. The five-week structure makes this an ideal choice during the season of Lent.

The material is planned for weekly gatherings. The meeting place could be at church or in homes. The key will be finding a place where everyone can feel safe as they share, reflect, and pray together.

This study is ideal for rotational leadership. As leaders and participants discover increased connection between worship and study, the understanding of leadership will continue to broaden. If a pastor is a part of your group, include him or her in the rotation. The opportunity to operate as a participant will be welcomed.

Adults of all ages and stages will find this study useful—singles groups, men's breakfasts, mom's time out, and new member study are just a few ideas. Because of the universality of the hymns used in this series, a young adult group may be as vital as an older adult group.

Planning each session

Gathering for the story

The first three pages of each session introduce the hymn. The instructions invite you to transition from a time of fellowship as you arrive, to gathering your thoughts about the hymn, checking in with each other, and then experiencing the hymn (see page 6), and finally prayer together.

Learning the story

This section provides relevant information about the text, the tune, and the legends of each hymn. The intent is not in-depth study, but an opportunity to discover stories and anecdotes about the persons and circumstances that were a part of the creation of the hymn.

Our story

Hymns and songs carry emotional and cognitive memories. In this section, you will be asked to reflect on how the hymn has been part of your growth in the Christian faith. The questions, similar in all sessions, provide time and a safe opportunity to share how the music and poetry has affected who we are as believers.

The biblical story

Unless the hymn writer indicated a specific biblical passage, the intended textual connection can never be certain. The writer of this study discovered textual connections and images for one stanza of each hymn and has provided questions to help you search for personal meaning related to faith traditions and the Bible.

Texts were selected from the New Revised Standard Version of the Bible (NRSV), but each participant may use his or her own Bible. Using a variety of translations can bring new perspectives to your discussions.

Additional questions to reflect on in this section of the study are:

- What is normally taken for granted about this passage?
- What is related to your own journey of faith?
- What connections to biblical and doctrinal understanding do you find?
- What may affect you personally in this text?

Living the story

Each hymn ends with three questions addressing how this hymn will affect the way you live your faith as a result of your learning. What message will you bring to each day?

Each session ends with praying and singing. The closing prayer, with time for individual petitions, and singing weave new dimensions to the hymn's familiar words and images.

Experiencing the hymn

An important part of this study is the experience of singing. Whether your group is large or small, raise your voices together each week. If a piano and accompanist are available, look for the full score in your favorite hymnal. All hymns are included in *Lutheran Book of Worship* or *With One Voice*, as well as in most traditional Christian hymnals.

If your group has instrumentalists, invite them to play with you as you sing. Perhaps someone's hidden talent will shine! Invite a young person or two from your congregation who play in their school orchestra or band to play along for one session.

Many of the hymns in the Sing the Faith volumes appear on numerous recordings. The reference list on page 47 offers a starting place for your search. You might publicize your study in your church newsletter or bulletin by listing the hymns and asking for recording recommendations. In addition, piano collections that include one or more of the hymns are suggested on this page.

Whether you sing *a cappella* or with a pipe organ at its fullest, enjoy your time with the music, with the texts, with memories of the past and hope for the future, and with each other as together you Sing the Faith.

Were You There

Text: African American spiritual, alt.
Music: WERE YOU THERE, African American spiritual

GATHERING FOR THE STORY

Greet participants as they arrive. Invite them to record their responses to this question in their book.

Do you remember a difficult moment in your life when you felt God's presence?

A Bible concordance would be a helpful tool for people who want to list text citations or search for stories by key words.

Do you remember being present and helpful to someone who was suffering?

Begin with introductions. Ask volunteers to share the stories they selected, then say the prayer together.

Have you ever felt abandoned or a tremendous loneliness?

Invite the group to sing "Were You There" (see page 7). Since this hymn is well suited to four-part singing, encourage participants who are able to sing the choral parts. See page 6 for more information.

(10 minutes)

Loving God,
Sometimes we need to know you are with us.
Sometimes we are lonely, afraid, and in pain.
Gives us the grace to know your presence in the
  lonely and difficult moments.
Give us the courage to help those in need
  and the grace to love all people.
May we love our neighbors as we love ourselves
  and be there for them as you are here for us.
Grant this through Christ our Lord. Amen

Were You There

Were you there when they crucified my Lord?
Were you there when they crucified my Lord?
Oh, sometimes it causes me to tremble, tremble, tremble.
Were you there when they crucified my Lord?

Were you there when they nailed him to the tree?
Were you there when they nailed him to the tree?
Oh, sometimes it causes me to tremble, tremble, tremble.
Were you there when they nailed him to the tree?

Were you there when they pierced him in the side?
Were you there when they pierced him in the side?
Oh, sometimes it causes me to tremble, tremble, tremble.
Were you there when they pierced him in the side?

Were you there when the sun refused to shine?
Were you there when the sun refused to shine?
Oh, sometimes it causes me to tremble, tremble, tremble.
Were you there when the sun refused to shine?

Were you there when they laid him in the tomb?
Were you there when they laid him in the tomb?
Oh, sometimes it causes me to tremble, tremble, tremble.
Were you there when they laid him in the tomb?

Text: African American spiritual, alt.

Learning the Story

After participants read the background of this hymn, talk about information they found meaningful or helpful.
(5 minutes)

The text

The style and text of African American spirituals are quite simple. Simplicity has a lot of merit and often points to very complex truth and reality. In "Were You There," there is an exquisite use of repetition that causes the singer or the hearer to pay close attention. Jesus' passion and death get summed up and repeated simply and poignantly. Then the chorus calls all who sing and listen to move beyond the beauty of the words into the reality of the pain. "Tremble, tremble, tremble" reminds all who would hear to tremble at Jesus' suffering, the suffering of others and one's own suffering.

The legend

This spiritual remains one of the most popular Lenten songs. Churches throughout America and the rest of the world have used it to reflect on the agony, suffering, and death of Jesus. During slavery, the slaves learned about the suffering of the Israelites and the suffering of Jesus. The more they learned about Christianity, the more they could identify with the suffering of Jesus. Here was Jesus, the innocent Son of God, condemned to death and killed. The slaves must have wondered why Jesus was abandoned by his friends and abandoned by God. Where were Jesus' friends, and where was God? As they thought over this troubling question and reflected on their experiences, they asked the question first to each other, to their masters, and to the rest of the world. Were you there?

Our Story

When was the first time you heard this spiritual?

> You may need to adapt these questions for the participants in your group. Ask them to record their responses and then share their stories.
> *(10 minutes)*

Where is God in your life in moments of suffering?

What does this spiritual encourage you to do?

The Biblical Story

Invite participants to find the passages in their Bibles and record their responses to the questions.

Were you there when they crucified my Lord?

Mark 14:49-50

Why is it so easy to abandon Jesus or our faith in hard times?

What do you think Jesus felt as he saw his friends abandon him?

Were you there when they nailed him to the tree?

Psalm 1:1-3

What graces, gifts, or new life have you experienced during moments of suffering?

Have you been able to find God in all moments of your life?

Were you there when they pierced him in the side?
John 19:31-34

What role do your baptism and Holy Communion play in your life?

What does it mean to be the body of Jesus in the world?

Were you there when the sun refused to shine?
Isaiah 9:1

During dark and difficult moments, where do you find grace and light?

What gives you hope?

Were you there when they laid him in the tomb?
Romans 6:1-4

Does death scare you? Why or why not?

How does the reality of death affect your Christian witness?

Determine if your group would prefer to:
◆ read and respond to all passages and questions before talking
◆ read, respond, and discuss one passage at a time
(20 minutes)

LIVING THE STORY

Invite participants to reflect for a few moments on today's conversation, and then respond to the questions. It is important to share the responses to these questions, so your group can offer prayer support to each other throughout the week.

Select a leader for your next meeting and remind everyone of the time and location.

Close by singing "Were You There" and praying together.

(10 minutes)

How does this spiritual challenge you to be aware of your suffering and the suffering of others?

We often miss the suffering of others because we do not see or hear them. How can you better be God's presence of healing and consolation in the world today or this week?

Is there something you can do this week to make life better for someone?

> Loving God,
>   you call us to be present to each other—
>   to be there when we are needed.
> Help us to serve the poor, the needy, the sick,
>   and the less fortunate.
> Give us eyes so that we may see our neighbor.
> Give us ears that we may hear them.
> Deepen our love for you
>   as we love and serve each other.
> Grant this through Christ our Lord. Amen

Swing Low, Sweet Chariot

1. I looked o-ver Jor-dan, and what did I see, coming for to car-ry me home? A band of an-gels coming af-ter me, coming for to car-ry me home.
2. If you get there be-fore I do, coming for to car-ry me home; tell all my friends I'm com - ing too, coming for to car-ry me home.
3. The bright-est day that ev-er I saw, coming for to car-ry me home; when Je-sus washed my sins a - way, com-ing for to car-ry me home.
4. I'm some-times up, I'm some-times down, coming for to car-ry me home; but still my soul feels heav-en-ly bound, com-ing for to car-ry me home.

Text: African American spiritual
Music: SWING LOW, African American spiritual

Gathering for the Story

Greet participants as they arrive. Invite them to record their responses to this question in their book.

A Bible concordance would be a helpful tool for people who want to list text citations or search for stories by key words.

Begin with introductions. Ask volunteers to share the stories they selected, then say the prayer together.

Invite the group to sing "Swing Low, Sweet Chariot" (see page 15). Since this hymn is well suited to four-part singing, encourage participants who are able to sing the choral parts. See page 6 for more information.

(10 minutes)

What makes you feel that you belong to God?

What makes you feel at home?

Can you remember an experience where you felt that God was watching over you?

Loving God,
   you are always with us
   and you rescue us when we need your help.
At times we are besieged by the pressures of life:
   we feel low, lost, and hopeless.
Over and over again, you remind us
   that love is stronger than hate
   and life more powerful than death.
Give us the grace to be loving, kind, and merciful.
Help us to trust you in difficult moments.
Help us to help others so that we may be a sign
   of hope, faith, and love for others.
Grant this through Christ our Lord. Amen

Swing Low, Sweet Chariot

Swing low, sweet chariot,
coming for to carry me home.
Swing low, sweet chariot,
coming for to carry me home.

I looked over Jordan, and what did I see,
coming for to carry me home?
A band of angels coming after me,
coming for to carry me home. Refrain

If you get there before I do,
coming for to carry me home;
tell all my friends I'm coming too,
coming for to carry me home. Refrain

The brightest day that ever I saw,
coming for to carry me home;
when Jesus washed my sins away,
coming for to carry me home. Refrain

I'm sometimes up, I'm sometimes down,
coming for to carry me home;
but still my soul feels heavenly bound,
coming for to carry me home. Refrain

Text: African American spiritual

LEARNING THE STORY

After participants read the hymn background, talk about information they found meaningful or helpful. (5 minutes)

The text

There is a beauty in the simplicity in the words of this spiritual. "Coming for to carry me home" deviates from our strict grammatical construction. Preserved in its original form, it proclaims the desire of those still oppressed.

Repetition is used to hammer home the theme of displacement. This is not our home, the singers proclaim. Notice the third verse and the use of a kind of assonance, an off-rhyme. The singers attempt to rhyme "saw" and "sins away." These two lines show how Jesus' actions lead to a separation from sin, taking sin away from the sight of the slaves. The same Jesus who takes their sin away will take them away to their true home. Verse four uses "down" to rhyme with "bound" — the slaves were bound, but more importantly they were bound for heaven.

The legend

Many have suggested that the spirituals held secret messages, and it is possible that the emphasis on being taken home was a cry or reminder that the plantation owner was not home and there was need to steal away.

In this spiritual, there is a reference to the Old Testament story of Elijah being taken up into heaven, a band of angels, and the redemptive act of Jesus. God has a home for the slaves and they feel confident that the chariot will take them home. So deep is their misery and so low is their estate that the chariot will need to swing low.

OUR STORY

As you sing or listen to this hymn, what comes to mind?

> You may need to adapt these questions for the participants in your group. Ask them to record their responses and then share their stories.
> *(10 minutes)*

What makes you feel up and what makes you feel down spiritually?

"When Jesus washed my sins away..." What does this line say to you?

THE BIBLICAL STORY

Invite participants to find the passages in their Bibles and record responses to the questions.

Swing low, sweet chariot, coming for to carry me home
2 Kings 2:9-15

What does it mean to be taken up to heaven?

What made Elijah worthy of such special treatment by God?

I looked over Jordan, and what did I see…?
Matthew 3:13-17

How do you live out your baptismal vows to reject all that is evil?

If you get there before I do… Tell all my friends I'm coming too
Luke 23:39-43

How do you live your future hope?

When Jesus washed my sins away
Matthew 9:1-8

What does the gift of having one's sins washed away mean to you?

Determine if your group would prefer to:
◆ read and respond to all passages and questions before talking
◆ read, respond, and discuss one passage at a time
(20 minutes)

How do you experience God's forgiveness, and how do you forgive others?

I'm sometimes up, I'm sometimes down
Job 1:8-12, 20-22

Where in your life do you experience God's blessings?

When you are feeling down, what is your experience of God?

Swing Low, Sweet Chariot ◆ 21

LIVING THE STORY

Invite participants to reflect for a few moments on today's conversation, and then respond to the questions. It is important to share the responses to these questions, so your group can offer prayer support to each other throughout the week.

Select a leader for your next meeting and remind everyone of the time and location.

Close by singing "Swing Low, Sweet Chariot" and praying together.

(10 minutes)

How does this spiritual challenge your prayer life?

What is this hymn trying to tell you about how you live your life?

How can you be present to someone in his or her moment of need?

O God,
   come dwell in our hearts.
Teach us to make our home in you
   and give us the grace to rest in you.
Help us to care for the stranger,
   the homeless, the poor,
   and the troubled in our midst.
May we never forget that whatever
   we do for others
   we do to you.
Give us the grace to love you
   in good times and bad.
Grant this through your Son,
   our Savior, Jesus the Lord. Amen

This Little Light of Mine

1 This little light of mine, I'm goin'-a let it shine;
2 Ev-'ry-where I go, I'm goin'-a let it shine;
3 Je-sus gave it to me, I'm goin'-a let it shine;

this little light of mine, I'm goin'-a let it shine;
ev-'ry-where I go, I'm goin'-a let it shine;
Je-sus gave it to me, I'm goin'-a let it shine;

this little light of mine, I'm goin'-a let it shine,
ev-'ry-where I go, I'm goin'-a let it shine,
Je-sus gave it to me, I'm goin'-a let it shine,

let it shine, let it shine, let it shine.
let it shine, let it shine, let it shine.
let it shine, let it shine, let it shine.

Text: African American spiritual
Music: LET IT SHINE, African American spiritual

GATHERING FOR THE STORY

Greet participants as they arrive. Invite them to record their responses to this question in their book.

A Bible concordance would be a helpful tool for people who want to list text citations or search for stories by key words.

Begin with introductions. Ask volunteers to share the stories they selected, then say the prayer together.

Invite the group to sing "This Little Light of Mine" (see page 23). Since this hymn is well suited to four-part singing, encourage participants who are able to sing the choral parts. See page 6 for more information.

(10 minutes)

How are you called to shine your light?

Where are the areas of darkness in your life, the church, and society?

What does it mean to be given a light by Jesus?

> Eternal God, you are our light
>   and in you there is no darkness.
> Illumine our heart, mind, and soul
>   so that we may serve you
>   and bring the good news to others.
> Help us to lead others to you
>   and give us the gifts
>   of faithfulness and discernment.
> All this we ask in Jesus' name. Amen

This Little Light of Mine

This little light of mine, I'm goin'-a let it shine;
this little light of mine, I'm goin'-a let it shine;
this little light of mine, I'm goin'-a let it shine,
let it shine, let it shine, let it shine.

Ev'rywhere I go, I'm goin'-a let it shine;
ev'rywhere I go, I'm goin'-a let it shine;
ev'rywhere I go, I'm goin'-a let it shine,
let it shine, let it shine, let it shine.

Jesus gave it to me, I'm goin'-a let it shine;
Jesus gave it to me, I'm goin'-a let it shine;
Jesus gave it to me, I'm goin'-a let it shine,
let it shine, let it shine, let it shine.

Text: African American spiritual

LEARNING THE STORY

After participants read the hymn background, talk about information they found meaningful or helpful. (5 minutes)

The text

This spiritual could be paraphrased this way: "Jesus gave the light to me and everywhere I go, I will shine." The basic theme is repeated over and over again; perhaps this song could be the spiritual mantra of the 21st century. The line "Jesus gave it to me" employs the only use of the past tense. Interestingly enough, it is the last line in the spiritual, and the order of the lines is not accidental. There is a strong sense in the spiritual that everything is built upon the saving act of Jesus. With this final line, the singers confirmed their faith. The light is from Jesus, hope is from Jesus, and freedom will eventually come from Jesus. "Mine" rhymes with "shine," a great way of showing that the light is mine to shine. Simplicity rules in the economy of words that point to a deep insight of one's relationship with God.

The legend

This song is one of the most beloved songs of children. They sing it earnestly and with great joy, and their little voices speak of the possibilities of bringing light to the world. In the darkness of slavery, light must have taken on great importance. As the slaves learned about Christianity, they must have identified a call not only to draw close to the light, but to be the light. Once again, we encounter a determination to be good, to be strong, to be free, and to be light. "I'm goin' a let it shine." Surely they must have tried to live the Christian principles among each other. We can imagine the sacrifices, the acts of kindness, the selfless actions, and the hope they passed on to each other as a way of shining their light.

Our Story

When was the first time you heard or sang this song?

Recall a time when you felt proud or afraid that you were a Christian.

What have you learned from your family or church community that helps you to shine your light?

What does this spiritual say to you?

You may need to adapt these questions for the participants in your group. Ask them to record their responses and then share their stories.
(10 minutes)

The Biblical Story

Invite participants to find the passages in their Bibles and record responses to the questions.

This little light of mine
Matthew 5:14-16

What does this mean? How do Jesus' words make you feel?

I'm goin' a let it shine
John 9:1-12, 35-41

How do others see the light of Christ in you?

How does Christ's light get manifested through you?

Let it shine
Exodus 34:27-35

When have you ever had an experience like that of Moses? Share.

Have you ever felt filled with God's light?

Ev'ry where I go
Matthew 28:16-20

Where is God sending you?

Where are you called to take the light of Christ?

Jesus gave it to me
John 1:1-9

You may have received a lighted candle at your baptism. Where do you receive God's light these days?

How do you tap into God's grace and light each day?

Determine if your group would prefer to:
◆ read and respond to all passages and questions before talking
◆ read, respond, and discuss one passage at a time
(20 minutes)

LIVING THE STORY

Invite participants to reflect for a few moments on today's conversation, and then respond to the questions. It is important to share the responses to these questions, so your group can offer prayer support to each other throughout the week.

Select a leader for your next meeting and remind everyone of the time and location.

Close by singing "This Little Light of Mine" and praying together.

(10 minutes)

How does this spiritual call you to examine the way you live your life?

Where are you being called to claim grace, faith, and Christian responsibility?

What are some specific things you can do or say to show the light of Christ in your family, school, work, or church?

> God of light, God of grace,
>   we praise you for the ways
>   you bring light to our path
>   and grace for the journey.
> We praise you because
>   darkness can never overcome the light
>   and your grace is always greater
>   than our weakness and despair.
> Send us out into the world
>   as ministers of your way, grace, and light,
>   that we may be hope and light for others.
> Grant this through Jesus Christ our Lord. Amen

Let Us Break Bread Together

Text: African American spiritual
Music: BREAK BREAD TOGETHER, African American spiritual

GATHERING FOR THE STORY

Greet participants as they arrive. Invite them to record their responses to this question in their book.

A Bible concordance would be a helpful tool for people who want to list text citations or search for stories by key words.

Begin with introductions. Ask volunteers to share the stories they selected, then say the prayer together.

Invite the group to sing "Let Us Break Bread Together" (see page 31). Since this hymn is well suited to four-part singing, encourage participants who are able to sing the choral parts. See page 6 for more information.

(10 minutes)

Do you remember the first time you received communion? Share.

Who first taught you to pray?

What is different about your prayer as a child and as an older person?

> Eternal God, creator of all peoples:
>   we know you in and through
>   the gifts of each other
>   and we make you known by how we love others.
> As we gather, may we continue to know you
>   in the breaking of bread.
> As we gather in daily prayer,
>   break open the scriptures for us.
> Grant all this through Christ our Lord. Amen

Let Us Break Bread Together

Let us break bread together on our knees;
let us break bread together on our knees.

Refrain
When I fall on my knees,
with my face to the rising sun,
O Lord, have mercy on me.

Let us drink wine together on our knees;
let us drink wine together on our knees. *Refrain*

Let us praise God together on our knees;
let us praise God together on our knees. *Refrain*

Text: African American spiritual

LEARNING THE STORY

After participants read the hymn background, talk about information they found meaningful or helpful. (5 minutes)

The text

"Let us ..." opens this spiritual and is echoed throughout, setting a tone of gentleness and invitation. The invitation to worship and participate in communion is one of gentleness that stands in stark contrast to the brutality and insults so common to the slave experience. To break bread has an implicit contrast to the hardships of the broken lives of the slaves. Breaking bread, drinking wine, and praising God on bended knees all revolve around the theme of the rising sun. The sun could well be a reference to the lordship of Jesus. The sun, which follows the darkness, must have given them hope. It is as if worship gives strength to endure the rest of the day with all its troubles.

The legend

This text speaks of a humility that is both touching and inspiring. These days we can forget how awesome God is and this text serves as a gentle reminder. It also promotes the need to worship as a family or a community. It is an invitation to join in the breaking of bread. Slaves were not generally allowed to worship in the white churches and, in the rare moments that they were allowed, they were sent to the back of the church. But they grew in their love for Jesus and an understanding that God would have mercy on them. The spiritual reminds us all how seriously the slaves took their worship. In a unique way, this spiritual is a blueprint of and for worship.

OUR STORY

How do you prepare for communion?

> You may need to adapt these questions for the participants in your group. Ask them to record their responses and then share their stories.
> *(10 minutes)*

What postures do you use when you pray?

What were some of the prayers you learned as a child?

The Biblical Story

Invite participants to find the passages in their Bibles and record responses to the questions.

Let us break bread together on our knees
Luke 24:25-35

How do you "know Jesus" in the breaking of the bread?

When I fall on my knees, with my face to the rising sun
Colossians 4:2-6

How can you persevere in prayer?

O Lord, have mercy on me.
Mark 5:25-34

When have you needed or experienced the mercy of God?

Let us drink wine together on our knees
1 Corinthians 11:23-33

What witness does our sharing in the Lord's Supper give to the world?

Determine if your group would prefer to:
◆ read and respond to all passages and questions before talking
◆ read, respond, and discuss one passage at a time
(20 minutes)

Let us praise God together on our knees
John 4:19-26

Where are the holy places in our life?

What is true worship of God?

LIVING THE STORY

Invite participants to reflect for a few moments on today's conversation, and then respond to the questions. It is important to share the responses to these questions, so your group can offer prayer support to each other throughout the week.

Select a leader for your next meeting and remind everyone of the time and location.

Close by singing "Let Us Break Bread Together" and praying together.

(10 minutes)

How can this hymn affect your daily prayer?

Where in your life do you need to experience God's mercy or be an agent of mercy?

How do you feed on God's word?

> Loving God,
>   you give us all we have
>   and you provide all the things we need.
> Continue to give us the grace to know you.
> Encourage us in our desires
>   to know you in community.
> As we care for each other
>   may we continue to know you
>   in the breaking of the bread.
> Amen

I Want Jesus to Walk With Me

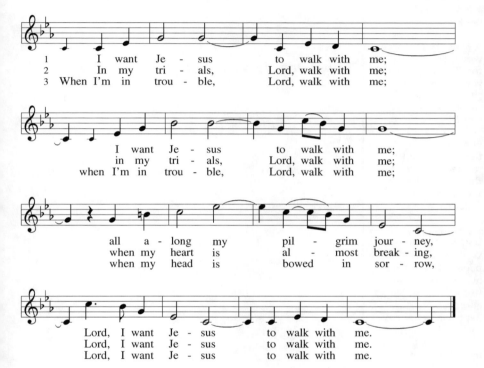

Text: African American spiritual
Music: SOJOURNER, African American spiritual

Gathering for the Story

Greet participants as they arrive. Invite them to record their responses to this question in their book.

A Bible concordance would be a helpful tool for people who want to list text citations or search for stories by key words.

Begin with introductions. Ask volunteers to share the stories they selected, then say the prayer together.

Invite the group to sing "I Want Jesus to Walk With Me" (see page 39). Since this hymn is well suited to four-part singing, encourage participants who are able to sing the choral parts. See page 6 for more information.

(10 minutes)

What do you want from Jesus?

What does Jesus want from you?

How do you experience Jesus walking with you?

> Lord Jesus, we are your pilgrim people
>   and you are our shepherd.
> Walk with us along life's journey
>   and help us to know your presence.
> When we are in trouble, give us peace,
>   give us solace,
>   and give us the gift of faithfulness.
> We pray in your holy name. Amen

I Want Jesus to Walk With Me

*I want Jesus to walk with me;
I want Jesus to walk with me;
all along my pilgrim journey,
Lord, I want Jesus to walk with me.*

*In my trials, Lord, walk with me;
in my trials, Lord, walk with me;
when my heart is almost breaking,
Lord, I want Jesus to walk with me.*

*When I'm in trouble, Lord, walk with me;
when I'm in trouble, Lord, walk with me;
when my head is bowed in sorrow,
Lord, I want Jesus to walk with me.*

Text: African American spiritual

LEARNING THE STORY

After participants read the hymn background, talk about information they found meaningful or helpful. (5 minutes)

The text
Teachers of creative writing often say that the first line sets the tone and essence of any work. This spiritual manages to capture the whole of the Christian message in the first three words: "I want Jesus." The singers employ a repetition at the beginning and end, thereby stressing that only one thing is important, and that is to want Jesus. This spiritual is at once a song, a poem, and a prayer. The brevity in the song shows the pain of the singer and the singer's trust in God.

The legend
One of the greatest signs of discipleship is the desire that Jesus journey with us. This spiritual may well have grown out of the Good Friday observances practiced by the early Christian missionaries or followers. In those days, the Lenten celebrations were more elaborate in some religions and the slaves might have seen reenactments of Jesus' passion. They wanted Jesus to walk with them because they identified with him and believed that he could understand them. Another sign of discipleship is the desire to have Jesus be present with us in our pain. Note the maturity of faith: the plea is not to have Jesus take the pain away, but to have Jesus walk with them.

Our Story

What do you want from God?

You may need to adapt these questions for the participants in your group. Ask them to record their responses and then share their stories. (10 minutes)

Does this song remind you of a painful moment or phase in your life? When?

How would you complete the line "I want Jesus to ..."?

THE BIBLICAL STORY

Invite participants to find the passages in their Bibles and record responses to the questions.

I want Jesus to walk with me
All along my pilgrim journey
John 1:35-39

If Jesus were to ask you what you want, what would be your response?

Lord, I want Jesus to walk with me
Matthew 19:21-24

What causes us to turn away from our spiritual desires?

In my trials, Lord walk with me
Matthew 10:16-25

How do you represent Jesus to those who suffer?

Where do you find spiritual strength when you suffer?

When my heart is almost breaking
1 Samuel 1:9-19
How does God suffer along with us?

How does God understand our suffering?

When my head is bowed in sorrow
Lord, I want Jesus to walk with me.
John 19:31-37
Can you share an experience of God's presence in the midst of suffering?

Determine if your group would prefer to:
◆ read and respond to all passages and questions before talking
◆ read, respond, and discuss one passage at a time
(20 minutes)

LIVING THE STORY

Invite participants to reflect for a few moments on today's conversation, then respond to the questions. It is important to share the responses to these questions so your group can offer prayer support to each other throughout the week.

Since this is the last session, take a few minutes to talk about future study this group might want to pursue.

Close by singing, "I Want Jesus to Walk With Me," or you may wish to sing all five hymns from *Spirituals*.

(10 minutes)

What does this spiritual say to you about discipleship?

What does Jesus want from you?

Where are you on the spiritual path these days?

> Loving God,
>   be our shepherd along the way,
>   be our companion day by day.
> Help us to trust that you walk with us.
> Give us the courage to walk with others,
>   and may we follow you ever more closely.
> Amen

RESOURCES

Choral Music

I Want Jesus to Walk With Me, arr. Bruce Trinkley. Augsburg Fortress Publishers (ISBN 0-8006-5707-1). To order call 1-800-328-4648 or go to www.augsburgfortress.org/store.

Were You There? arr. Richard Proulx. Augsburg Fortress Publishers (ISBN 0-8006-5451-X). To order call 1-800-328-4648 or go to www.augsburgfortress.org/store.

Instrumental Music

At the Foot of the Cross: Piano for the Lenten Journey, Jeremy Young. "Were You There." Augsburg Fortress Publishers (ISBN 0-8006-5539-7). To order call 1-800-328-4648 or go to www.augsburgfortress.org/store.

Come Away to the Skies: A Collection for Piano, Thomas Keesecker. "I Want Jesus to Walk With Me." Augsburg Fortress Publishers (0-8066-5655-5). To order call 1-800-328-4648 or go to www.augsburgfortress.org/store.

Jazz Lenten Journey, Michael Hassell. "Were You There." Augsburg Fortress Publishers (ISBN 0-8006-5949-X). To order call 1-800-328-4648 or go to www.augsburgfortress.org/store.

Piano Arrangement for Worship: Lent/Easter, Sara Glick. "I Want Jesus to Walk With Me." Augsburg Fortress Publishers (ISBN 0-8006-5880-9). To order call 1-800-328-4648 or go to www.augsburgfortress.org/store.

Reflections on Hymn Tunes for Holy Communion, arr. Anne Krentz Orgon. "Let Us Break Bread Together." Augsburg Fortress Publishers (ISBN 0-8006-5497-8). To order call 1-800-328-4648 or go to www.augsburgfortress.org/store.

This Little Light of Mine: Piano Collection, arr. J. Bert Carlson. "This Little Light of Mine." Augsburg Fortress Publishers (ISBN 0-8006-5950-3). To order call 1-800-328-4648 or go to www.augsburgfortress.org/store.

Traveling Tunes (Hymn Arrangements for Solo Instrument and Piano), Michael Hassell. "I Want Jesus to Walk With Me." Augsburg Fortress Publishers (ISBN 0-8006-5619-9). To order call 1-800-328-4648 or go to www.augsburgfortress.org/store.

Were You There? (for organ and flute), arr. Paul A. Nicholson. Augsburg Fortress Publishers (ISBN 0-8006-5408-0). To order call 1-800-328-4648 or go to www.augsburgfortress.org/store.

Recorded Music

Dusting Off the Green Book ("Let Us Break Bread Together"). Tom Witt, Concordia 6000011229.

Folk Songs, Spirituals, & Hymns ("This Little Light of Mine"). Concordia Choir, Concordia 6000143192.

The Spirituals of William Dawson ("Swing Low, Sweet Chariot"). St. Olaf Choir. To order, call 507-646-3646 or e-mail music@stolaf.edu.